MY
LUCKY
CUSTOMER

Also by Alexandria Blaelock

SHORT STORY COLLECTIONS
The Histories of Hayward Hall
Lovelorn, Lovestruck and Love at First Sight
Common or Garden Variety Heroes
Case Files of the Wilkinson Detective Agency
Unavoidable Fates
Christmas Travesties
Five Faces of Felicia Clarke
Little Place Called Home
Security Directorate Dossiers v. 1.
Security Directorate Dossiers v. 2.

FICTION
That Love Nonsense
Taipan vs Brown
The Ghost and Ms Cox
Friends Like That
Weaving the Wildwood
Wolf vs Orb

MS BLAELOCK'S BOOKS
Stress Free Dinner Parties
Signature Wardrobe Planning
Holistic Personal Finance
Minimally Viable Housekeeping
Planning a Life Worth Living

PICTURE BOOKS
Australia Felix

SELECTED SHORT STORIES
Alma's Grace
Blood and Bloody Profanity
Cancelled by the Cartel
Dingo Hunting
Honoris Virilis Respectu
Mince Pie Mystery
Remains of Christmas

MY LUCKY CUSTOMER

A FELICIA CLARKE SHORT STORY

ALEXANDRIA BLAELOCK

BlueMere Books

MELBOURNE, AUSTRALIA

For permission requests, please contact enquiries@bluemerebooks.com.

Ordering Information:
Discounts are available on quantity purchases. For details, contact orders@bluemerebooks.com.

My Lucky Customer/Alexandria Blaelock
paperback ISBN: 978-1-922744-12-8
digital ISBN: 978-1-922744-13-5

Book Layout © BookDesignTemplates.com
Cover Art © Vladimir Arndt via depositphotos

MY LUCKY CUSTOMER

Erol stood on the street, key in hand, admiring the tiny shop he'd just signed the lease on.

Something he couldn't have conceived of as a boy during the war.

He'd barely thought past the very next minute; where to hide, where to get food, and whatever happened to the rest of his family.

Arriving in England and getting permission to stay was a miracle.

For years he'd worked five part-time, casual jobs, living week to week in a small room in a rooming house, eating leftovers from the plates at the restaurant he washed dishes in.

Saving all his money for this day.

The building itself was at least 200 years old, and the London yellow bricks had achieved a fairly uniform coating of black dust he couldn't do any-thing about.

It was the same shade as all the other buildings around it so it didn't stand out.

But the store frontage did.

Painted orange of all things.

So cheerful against the gloom he'd fallen in love with it.

He found the colour comforting as well, though he couldn't remember a time when something orange made him feel safe.

The London skies weren't as bright or clear as those he'd grown up with. Even in midsummer the sunshine painted the whole town in a muted watercolour grey wash.

The orange Edwardian style frontage surrounded two glass windows and a half glass door with kick plates at street level.

They were sandwiched between two plain, modern blue doors either side leading to the first and second story flats respectively.

The windows had a thin coat of whitewash, presumably to deter squatters, and he hoped it wouldn't be hard to get off; that the windows would actually clean.

He'd need all the light he could force into the shop!

He turned the key and opened the door, faced with a single open room, strewn with rubbish and in dire need of cleaning.

Though perhaps it wouldn't seem so bad once he'd washed the white off the windows.

Best of all, through a door to his right, stairs to a tiny basement.

There was no natural light from the street, so the zoning didn't permit residential, but as it included a rudimentary bathroom and kitchen, he planned to live there anyway.

He'd need all the hours of the day to get set up, and make his tiny business a success.

Erol wanted to immediately start ordering stock and fittings for the store, and perhaps one or two small pieces of furniture for the basement.

But first, logic required cleaning the place so he could move in.

He locked the door, and walked down to the DIY store, to buy some cleaning products and a measuring tape.

And then a few hours later, back to the DIY store to buy a small ladder, some paint and bits and pieces for the small repairs required.

Then later still, back to his digs to shower and change for his shift at the restaurant.

Only after his five hour shift did he manage to get to his computer to the second hand store supply company he'd bookmarked to order the furniture.

The best thing about ordering second hand, was next day delivery!

Or given it was very early in the morning, the day after.

Only then did he sleep.

Then packed his bags, turned in his rooming house keys, and set off for his new life without looking back.

Later that evening, he stood outside his orange store, surrounded by his bags and packages, enjoying the moment.

His very own tiny store!

"Are you lost?" a woman's voice asked.

He turned to see a middle aged woman wearing an old-fashioned navy blue skirt suit, carrying a bulging shopping bag over one arm.

She didn't seem to notice a lock of greying dark hair had escaped her bun and was twisted around her neck.

She looked tired. Worn out.

Erol smiled, hoping to lighten her load, seeing as she had stopped to ask if he was all right.

"No Ma'am, I'm admiring my new shop."

She put her bag down and turned to look at the empty shop. "Well, it certainly looks very clean. What will you be selling."

"It's a convenience store."

"Good choice. There's not much of that around here. If you stock pints of milk, half loaves of wholemeal, and Silk Cut in packs of ten I'll stop by every day."

"Thank you Ma'am, I'll certainly do that."

She smiled and picked up her bag, "when will you open?"

"Next week."

"Then I'll see you then."

He watched her walk past the next couple of shops before turning into the first street on the left.

He hoped she didn't have far to go, she looked dead on her feet.

When he got back inside, he took his bags down stairs, and came back with his string of lucky charms.

During the war, he'd given up on gods, and started reciting a list of every single piece of good luck that happened to him.

Once he got a little more settled, he started buying lucky charms to represent them. Erol figured they'd work as well as prayers, if not better.

Though in a way, they became a kind of string of prayer beads as he touched each charm while reciting the list.

It had grown into a good, thick string of charms, so it seemed to be working. He'd have to find another two charms to add now. One for the shop, and one for the lady.

He dragged the ladder over, and hung it from a hook in the ceiling. Like a shop bell; it would chime when someone opened the door.

Hopefully multiplying his blessings every time someone did.

He opened and shut the door a couple of times to make it ring.

It was going to be great.

But in the meantime, he had dishes to wash.

«« • »»

The next day, he was up early, restlessly pacing, waiting for the furniture to arrive.

To calm his nerves, in what would become part of his morning routine, he took his standing brush with the blue plastic pan and swept the street directly in front of his shop.

He heard footsteps trotting down the path and looked up to see yesterday's navy-suited woman walking down the street in the same blue suit, or one very like it.

"Good morning Ma'am," he said as she neared.

"And good morning to you," she replied, nodding as she walked past.

He watched her walk further down the street, thinking she must work very long hours.

No wonder she was so tired when she walked back again.

He wondered where she worked.

Before too long he'd invented a life for her, working in the City at a merchant bank or some such; always rushed off her feet.

He hoped they appreciated her, and treated her like the Lady he knew she was.

He sighed, thinking and hoping, that soon he'd be rushed off his feet as well.

Having swept the footpath, he went back inside, sitting on the floor with his laptop, to start ordering stock. Including milk in pints, bread in half loaves, but was disappointed for find he could only order cigarettes in packs of twenty.

Almost before he'd finished, the furniture started arriving, and he spent the day arranging, and rearranging the shelves and fridge around the walls, and carrying and arranging his living accommodations downstairs.

The local women and children watched him working, but ignored him as he greeted them.

He found the staring a little unnerving, but consoled himself that he had one regular customer already.

Much later, he was sitting on the doorstep, resting before heading to the restaurant when his navy-suited lady walked up to him, carrying a bulging shopping bag.

"How is it coming along?" she asked.

"Very well Ma'am. Some of the stock will start arriving in the morning."

"That's exciting for you."

"Yes."

"Well, I'll let you get on," she said, and kept walking.

Such a lady.

««　•　»»

The days flew past.

Stock came in, he arranged it in the shelves, flattened the boxes and packed them up to go out with the rubbish.

The navy suited lady walked down the road in the morning, and back up in the evening.

He was always outside ready to greet her.

He notified the restaurant he was leaving, but worked right up until the night before his shop opened.

«« • »»

The night before he opened, Erol was so excited, he barely slept a wink.

Driven out of bed early by nervous anticipation, he almost prayed for success, but recalled himself just in time, reciting his good luck list instead.

He got out of bed and climbed the stairs to check the store layout, one last time.

Were the right products in the right place?

Would it promote a good flow of traffic around the space?

Just about the time he was about to go mad with doubt, he heard a van slow outside, then two distinct thuds as the newspapers were thrown out, followed by a roar as the van sped off to its next stop.

He dragged the papers in and arranged them on the counter.

And then to calm himself, he started a new routine; dusting the cheap light fixtures hanging from the ceiling, then moving onto the cigarette displays and the cards of lighters, cheap toys and other bits and bobs hanging from the walls.

Moving onto the shelves and the goods on them, wiping down the refrigerated units, and spraying the counter with cleaner.

Finally, sweeping the floor. Edging his small broom under the wooden shelves, sweeping the dust, loose hairs and fluff into the pan.

And as the time of the blue-suited lady approached, out onto the street to sweep off the footpath.

"Good morning," she said, "are you open?"

"Yes Ma'am," and scurried to open the door for her, "what can I help you with?"

She walked past him into the store, taking a quick look around before meeting him at the counter.

"It's looking good, you should do well with what you've got," which was a load of his mind.

She continued, "I'll take *The Guardian* and a pack of Silk Cut."

He folded the paper in half, topped it with the cigarettes, apologising for the law having changed and not being permitted to sell packs of ten.

"I'm sorry," she said, "I'd forgotten." She handed over a £5 note, adding, "keep the change."

"Thank you Ma'am."

She turned to the door, then looked back at him, "what time do you shut?"

He smiled, "about the same time I see you walking back every day."

"Then see you later alligator," she said with a wink as she walked out the door.

He listened to the chiming charms, and grinned.

That his first customer should be his navy-suit lady was good luck.

That she told him to keep the change made him want to frame the note for more good luck.

«« • »»

Though by the end of the day, he was feeling as though his luck had run out.

He did not see one single other customer all day.

When his navy-suited lady arrived that evening, he was despondent.

"Cheer up," she said, placing her bread, milk and a tin of baked beans on the counter, "you're here now, they'll get here too. Just as soon as they start running out of things."

He mumbled something shameful and she laughed.

"It's only the first day! Half the street hasn't even figured out you're here yet. Why don't you put a poster in the window offering some opening week discounts? I'm sure that will bring people in."

And when he thought about it, that wasn't a bad idea.

He decided on discounting the bread and milk as it wasn't the kind of thing he could hold over for long.

$$\text{«« • »»}$$

Over the next few days, as customers started trickling in, the navy-suited lady encouraging him to start thinking about his little shop on a larger level.

It was more than just *his* little shop, it was a part of a community. And if he wanted to make a living, (and he did), he needed to make it his community.

His community was mostly the white English people who lived in the surrounding streets.

The few Asians were outliers, and he could stock a few things for them, but he didn't want to be seen as an Asian supermarket.

For his shop to be a success, he needed to stock the particular goods his community needed.

He made time to walk about the estate, looking at the flats and houses they lived in, and smelling the foods they cooked.

He visited the nearby stores and closest supermarkets where they might be shopping.

He even looked at the rubbish in the streets to see what he could learn from that.

When the children started coming in to spend their pocket money, he asked them about their favourite ice creams, crisps and sweets and made sure he ordered them in.

As their mother's started coming in, what sizes and brands of products they preferred.

And the men, what cigarettes and alcohol.

The whole thing terrified him; asking total strangers what they wanted, but he understood the need to get to know his people.

Some of them didn't take it well; "sod off you paki-bastard go back to where you came from and mind your own business."

But he learned and grew, got better at asking, and started getting better answers "oh, I've got five kids so always the biggest boxes of cereal."

And he remembered it all, "how are you and your five kids - I've got that cereal here for whenever you need it."

And through it all, the navy-suited woman was there, his first customer in the morning, and the last at night.

Offering her little bits of advice.

Consoling him on the rude customers.

And congratulating him on the best.

«« • »»

As the years progressed, his store became a place his community could rely on. He always had just what they needed, and nothing more.

Throughout it all, the navy-suited woman continued to be his best customer.

His ideal customer, about whom he remembered all the little snippets of information he learned about her.

That she walked to Kings Cross Station in the morning rather than Caledonian Road because it was easier for her to get on the tube.

After work she walked home via the supermarket, and when he discovered how many ready meals she ate, he started stocking her favourites for her convenience.

And after advertising their introduction with a poster in the window, was surprised at how popular they were with other customers.

As the local children grew older and ruder, she spoke to them, then marched them back inside to apologise to him.

Sometimes their parents would come in later to apologise as well.

It turned out she worked for a lawyer, and rarely made it out for lunch, so he started stocking ready made sandwiches.

Similarly, with a poster in the window, he started selling more of them too.

For every small change he made for her convenience, he was rewarded with a gain from his other customers.

«« • »»

One day, decades after he'd first met her, she came to tell him she was moving away.

"I have cancer. I'm moving North to be closer to my niece."

"Oh my," he said, "I'm so sorry. Is there anything I can do to to help."

She laughed; a strangely chilling sound, "there's nothing anyone can do now."

"I'm so sorry."

And he was. He wished there was something he could do.

He looked around the shop, trying to see something he could give her.

She turned to go.

"Wait!"

She turned back, watching him dash for the step ladder.

He carefully took the bulky string of lucky charms down, and offered it to her. "I think you might need this luck more than me."

Her hands dipped with the weight of the charm threaded strings.

"I can't take this," she said.

"Ma'am—"

"Felicia," she corrected, "it occurs to me that after more than twenty years, I haven't told you my name."

He smiled, not mentioning it had in fact been thirty-four years, seven months, and fifteen days.

He placed his hands under hers, supporting the weight of the charms in hers, "Felicia, consider for a moment, that over that time, I have taken your luck."

"Not at all. I have been lucky to have such a dedicated shopkeeper here in you."

"Almost all my luck has been yours," he said, and recited his list of good luck, counting the charms, stopping as he got to the first day he met her, showing her how much longer and thicker the string had become since he'd met her.

"Please take this," he said, putting one hand on his heart, "it's all in here anyway."

"All right," she said as she pulled the charm he'd bought when they first met from the strings. "Take this, and start a new string."

"I will," he said, clutching it so hard it bit into his hand.

"Good luck then."

"And you."

The door opened and closed silently.

He did not watch her walk away.

And he never saw her again.

But if he'd been a praying man, he would have prayed for her.

THE END

As a small token of my thanks for reading...

Please enjoy 10% off everything (excluding shipping)

at alexandriablaelock.com

with the code erolten.

Turn the page for some ideas where to use it,

IF YOU ENJOYED THIS STORY… Why
not try the collection

Felicia Clarke; influencer.

Old Fashioned. Fiercely independent.

Encourages others, but treads her own path.

Dead, but fondly remembered.

By some.

Get to know Felicaia through these five stories.

Do you have what it takes to be a hero?

Whether that's running into a burning building, standing up for what you know is right, or saving the Princess it's going to take everything you've got and more besides.

In this genre-spanning collection of original stories, five women draw on resources they didn't know they had.

Join them, if you dare.

Home is where the heart is

You can struggle to find the place you call home. It's not a place, it's a feeling. You'll know it when you find it.

This collection of short stories explores our search for a place we can call home.

Short, sweet and relatable, these stories will make you homesick for places you've never been.

Welcome to Wilkinson's

I'm afraid Mr Hall's running a little late, can I get you a tea or coffee while you wait?

No?

What if I tell you about some of the recent cases we've been involved in?

Get comfortable and settle in for a wild ride.

you go girl!
The opposite
of winning
isn't losing,
it's quitting.
· Martha Rosette Lutz ·
Time for
a nice cup
of tea and
a sit down
Time for
a nice cup
of tea and
a biscuit
There's a book for that

Time for a nice cup of tea
and a sit down
BEWARE THE EMPTINESS GREMLINS

Australian author Alexandria Blaelock writes mostly fantasy and mystery.

She's appeared in the Stringybark Anthology *Crowd Surfing*, *Pulphouse Fiction Magazine*, and *Ellery Queen's Mystery Magazine*.

She's also written five self-help books applying business techniques to personal matters like getting dressed, tidying up, and feeding friends.

Discover more at alexandriablaelock.com.

Get insider updates on my writing, advance notice of new releases, discounts, free ebooks, stories, and much, much more in my monthly communiqués.

Sign up at

alexandriablaelock.com/insider-updates